Buffy, thanks for all.
Much remains unsaid.
Oz

Buffy
thank you for the
talk in the tower
and for everything
Jonathan

Buffy,
I know moms don't usually
sign yearbooks, but I wanted
to let you know how proud
I am and how much I love
you.
Mom

Buffy Summers —
I take comfort in knowing
this school will stand
long after you leave it.
— Principal Snyder

Buffy-
you have been
a mystery
and a challenge.
More or less in
a good way.
- Wesley

BUFFY:
WILLOW TELLS ME
THAT TO INSCRIBE
THESE WORDS IS
TO PARTICIPATE
IN AN ANCIENT
RITUAL:
YOU'RE THE
SWEETEST.
DON'T EVER
CHANGE!
-ANYA

Dear Buffy,
I've spent much of my life making guesses as
to my father's opinion of me. There are times
when I've detected disappointment. Even a few
when I think I've recognized satisfaction.
I don't want you to have to guess what
I'm feeling as I watch you graduate.
This is pure pride—
Giles

Buffy- Just remember, clear gloss
over a warm color will help
you with that washed-out
cracked lip thing.
Harmony

BUFFMASTER-
YOU'RE the Bomb!
LARRY

SUNNYDALE
HIGH
YEARBOOK

SUNNYDALE HIGH YEARBOOK

Christopher Golden and Nancy Holder

POCKET BOOKS
New York   London   Toronto   Sydney   Tokyo   Singapore

For the Marian High School Class of 1985—C. G.

For the Class of 2015—N. H.

Christopher and Nancy would like to thank
Joss Whedon, Caroline Kallas, and the entire cast and crew of Buffy;
Debbie Olshan at Fox; our editor at Pocket, Lisa Clancy; assistant editor, Liz Shiflett;
Lisa's assistant, Micol Ostow; and the rest of the tireless Pocket team.

Christopher would like to thank
his agent, Lori Perkins, Cat Morgillo, and Connie and the boys.

Nancy would like to thank
her agent, Howard Morhaim; his assistant, Lindsey Sagnette;
the Baby-sitter Battalion; my husband, Wayne; and our beautiful daughter, Belle.

Special thanks to the following people:
Nancy Pines, Patricia MacDonald, Kathryn Briggs-Gordon, Jane Ginsberg, Donna O'Neill,
Julie Blattberg, Gina DiMarco, Anna Dorfman, Lisa Feuer, Linda Dingler,
Twisne Fan, Margaret Clark, Lili Schwartz, Jennifer Robinson,
and Jane Espenson for her contributions.

Yearbook Editor: Lisa A. Clancy
Yearbook Designer: Lili Schwartz

Video grabs courtesy of OnmiGraphic Solutions
Additional photography courtesy of MVP Media

This book is a work of fiction. Names, characters, places, and incidents are products of the author's imagination
or are used fictitiously. Any resemblance to actual events or locales or persons, living or dead, is entirely coincidental.

 POCKET BOOKS, a division of Simon & Schuster, Inc.
1230 Avenue of the Americas, New York, NY 10020

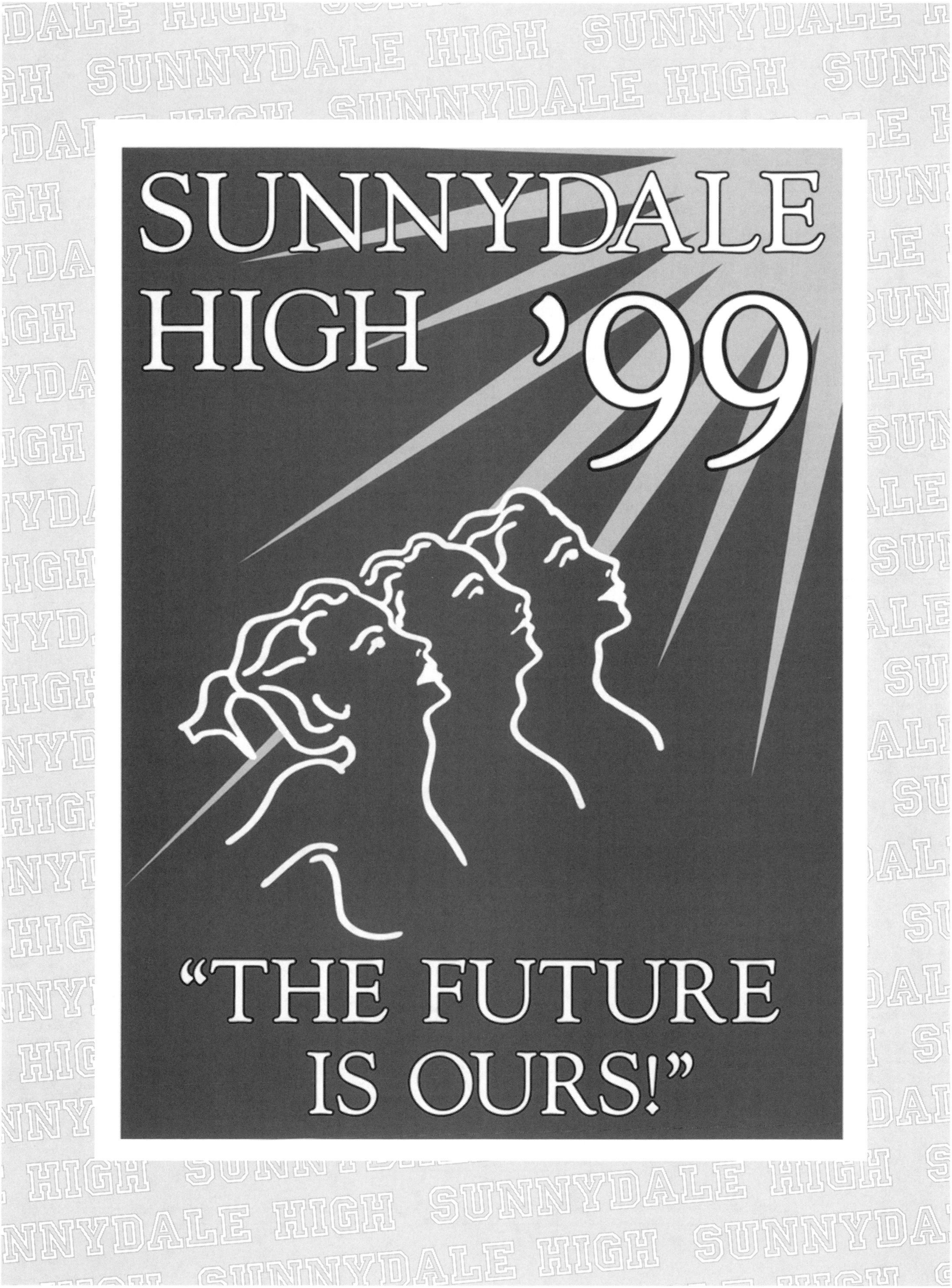
SUNNYDALE HIGH '99
"THE FUTURE IS OURS!"

Table of Contents

Sunnydale High School

A Message from the Mayor

To the Sunnydale High Class of 1999:

I'd like to take this opportunity to congratulate each and every one of you as you leave Sunnydale High School. I truly believe that you young people are bright shiny beacons of hope, guiding us toward the future. This is the dawning of a thrilling new era here on earth. It takes my breath away.

I consider myself a lucky man to be from Sunnydale, as generations of my family have been before me. I draw strength from this town and its people, strength that makes a man feel positively invulnerable. Maybe you also know how fortunate you are to be living here. Many are not.

I feel strangely as if I will be graduating with you, Razorbacks. Moving on to something new and exciting and clean. When you take hold of your diplomas, think of me, the oldest graduating member of the Class of 1999.

Richard Wilkins III
Mayor of Sunnydale

A Message from the Principal

Seniors,

I have never had as much pleasure at bidding good-bye to a graduating class as I have this year.

I have not been easy on you. Nor you on me. But it's over and we survived. Those of you reading this survived.

I wish you success that will draw you far away from your beginnings here. And if you should ever wish to return, to visit our humble building and your favorite teachers, remember that I enforce a strict visitor policy.

Whether you are moving on to employment, or to higher education, or perhaps to a continued life as your parents' dependent, the important thing is that you are leaving here.

Good-bye.
Principal R. Snyder

Sunnydale High School

This Certifies That

_____

Having completed the Course of Study prescribed by the Board of Education

and having the approved intellectual attainments and good conduct is hereby declared

a Graduate of this High School and is therefore entitled to receive this

Diploma

Given at Sunnydale, California, this month of June, nineteen hundred ninety nine.

_____
Principal of High School

_____
Superintendent of Schools

_____
Chairman of Board

_____
Secretary of Board

The Associated Student Body of
Sunnydale High School

presents

"Bridge Over Troubled Water"

Prom 1999

May 11 8:00 p.m.

Formal Attire

I wish I could have given all of you more moments like this.
—Giles

10

Buffy, to say the unsaid stuff I wrote a song. It's an instrumental. Oz

To Our Protector
by Jonathan Levenson

Those of you who attended this year's prom got to witness the presentation of a new award here at Sunnydale High. The "Class Protector" umbrella trophy was presented to Buffy Summers. It was not a very beautiful trophy, because I didn't have a lot of time, and nobody contributed as much money as they promised. But it was heartfelt. Buffy Summers has been our umbrella. Especially the pointy part on top.

Thank you, Buffy.

Who's cute now, mister English guy?

Lucky devil ———→
—Xander

HOMECOMING

Sunnydale Crowns Two Lovely Queens

Behold their majesties! As Devon MacLeish of the Dingoes asked for "the envelope, please!" he announced another first in S.H.S. history. The Sunnydale High student body chose *two* beautiful seniors to reign over them at Homecoming. This may have been the first time there has ever been a tie for Queen, but what a hard choice it was to vote from among all the candidates!

Queen Holly Charleston enjoys her second consecutive year on the Homecoming Court. She has been a member of the volleyball team for all four years. Holly is a well-known leader on campus and an active member of the Mayor's Youth Council. Her hopes for the future are to attend an Ivy League college and live happily ever after.

Queen Michelle Blake is a newcomer to the Homecoming Court. Recently transferred from Providence, Rhode Island, she is also a member of the Mayor's Youth Council. Her future plans are "to remain in Sunnydale for the rest of my life and marry someone with the initials S.H."

Escort Joe Nakamura was happy to pose with Queen Holly. The senior anticipates acceptance to Harvard, in preparation for medical school.

Escort Alex DuVallier squired Queen Michelle to her royal throne. After graduation, he will assume night manager duties at the Putter's Green Mini-Golf Course and attend Crestwood College in the fall.

Sunnydale Salutes Two Beautiful Runners Up

Beautiful senior Cordelia Chase, a member of Varsity Cheer, was May Queen last year. That in itself was quite an accomplishment for a junior. As a senior, Cordelia has graced many a school function with her style and grace.

Pretty senior Buffy Summers came to Sunnydale as a sophomore from Los Angeles and has managed to find a niche at S.H.S. She can often be seen hanging with her friends in the library or in the lounge.

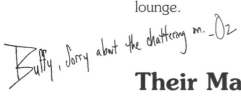

Their Majesties' Court

Juniors Katrina Giersch and Tracy Malcolm have both been on the Court before and were thrilled to wear the crowns of Junior Princesses.

Sharon Simonet and Jessica Morris were proud to be selected as the Sophomore Princesses. They hope to be princesses next year as well.

Being freshmen and princesses as well was very exciting for Jenny Naranjo and Susan Conklin.

Homecoming
Dance

A Fashion Perspective
by Harmony Kendall

The homecoming dance sets the fashion standard for the rest of the school year. This is a chance for the best of us to shine. But not just that. It's also a chance for us to study the less taste-equipped, to offer them guidance and constructive criticism. Then they, in turn, can pass it on to those too pathetic to even get asked to the dance. It's the circle of life.

This year's homecoming dance started out like a ray of golden hope into the dark world of the style-starved. The dresses, in general, left behind the ruffles and flounces of girlhood, and favored instead the sleek silhouettes of womanliness. All in all, the dance was a veritable gift basket of fashion-dos!

It was, that is, until Buffy Summers and Cordelia Chase arrived. With their artfully torn gowns, streaked faces, and tangled hair, they attempted to inject a kind of Courtney Love You-know-I'm-cool-because-I-look-like-trash sensibility into the proceedings. It was a fashion miscalculation of the highest order.

Jeers! Jeers, I say to Buffy and Cordelia for thumbing their oh-so-smudged noses at the fashion rule of law. Without fashion there is anarchy, and without Cordy and Buffy, there is fashion!

Why can't the yearbook have more stuff like this?

STUDENT LIFE

ACTIVITIES
& CLUBS

Band

Wow, what a year for the three divisions of the Sunnydale High School Band! It was a year with some extraordinary accomplishments all around, but the first thing we want to do is congratulate our members who will be going on to continue their musical studies at various performing arts and university-level music programs around the nation. Why, we have three graduates attending the Berklee School of Music alone. They are Caitlin Bryant, Doreen Albertson, and Jay Theron. Other seniors include Wendell Sears, Oz, Eric Gittleson, Mashad Bolling, and Lisa Campiti.

The band performed all year at school events, including the school's productions of *Oklahoma* and *A Chorus Line,* as well as accompanying several performers in the Talent Show.

The S.H.S. Jazz Band performed on Saturdays throughout the fall and spring at Hammersmith Park and became one of the highlights among the park's regular performances, raising money for the Runaways Fund and the Halley Carmichael Women's Shelter through charitable donations from the audience. Way to go, jazzers!

Finally, we had a great honor this year when the Sunnydale High School Razorbacks' Marching Band was invited to perform during half time at the November football game between the San Diego Chargers and the Atlanta Falcons. Thanks to Sunnydale's Mayor Wilkins for providing transportation to and from San Diego for our marchers.

Band Candy

Baby, baby, baby, baby!

Sunnydale got a real sugar "rush" when S.H.S. students sold big, luscious chocolate bars to raise money for new band uniforms. Some of the school's adult boosters got together to turn the Bronze into a real "Sugar Shack!" while they got their sweet teeth into such tasty oldies as "Louie Louie."

There should be a law against 'candid' snaps.
–Giles

"Mr. Giles! Are you trying out for *Grease*?"

FROM THE DESK OF

As director of the S.H.S. marching band, I am writing this open letter of gratitude to all those students who participated in the "Band Candy" fund-raising drive. I was shocked to learn that this year's sales totaled a massive $600,000 in profits! As our target was $1,500, I was pleased as punch! I have put this money to good use, purchasing new uniforms, two new sousa-phones, and a performing arts center.

Thanks!

A Thank You from the Marching Band Director

The Sentinel

S U N N Y D A L E   H I G H   S C H O O L

Not to be trite, but the truth *is* out there. And Freddy Iverson, editor of the *Sunnydale High Sentinel,* spent four years trying to find it. We've had some sad times and some frightening moments in our four years here, including the gang

Freddy often scopes out the student lounge to get the inside scoop!

attack during last year's Parent/Teacher Night, and Freddy and his team of reporters and columnists—Robert Stefanopoulos, Jonathan Levenson, Lance Lincoln, and Wendell Sears—were always there, searching for the truth, reporting the news, good and bad.

Freddy took his job very seriously, and the *Sentinel* was all the better for it. The staff of the *Sentinel* wanted to offer up a special thank you and acknowledgement to the man Freddy refers to as the paper's "number-one snitch throughout the year," the man who provided *Sentinel* reporters with the inside scoop when the authorities were silent, and who never failed to lend an opinion on where Sunnydale High was headed: Principal Snyder.

Who ever thought a school principal would be so cooperative in dishing the dirt for the school paper? But time and again, he was there for them with information they couldn't get anywhere else, revealing the real story—gang-related incidents, people under the influence of PCP, and the oft-backed-up sewer lines—when others made wild and ridiculous claims.

We can only hope Principal Snyder will continue in this spirit of cooperation with the paper's new editor next year.

Abandon Hope

As the final year of high school ends for the class of '99, I am reminded of a quote: "It gets worse from here." It was uttered by a great man, I forget who, when things were about to become worse. And although it is hard to believe, I am afraid that this quote is deadly accurate for those of us leaving S.H.S. As soul-destroying and intellect-crushing as high school was, it was only a taste of what the working world has lying in wait for us. At least, as we battled our way though the cruelty of our peers and the stupidity of our teachers, we knew that our tenure in this place was limited to four, or at most six, years. Now many of us will find ourselves dumped into the even hotter frying pan that is college and then the flesh-charring fire of permanent employment. At this stage we lose not only hope, but also our souls. They defeat us not by killing us, but by turning us into blank-eyed drones in the teeming anthill of life. I bid high school a fond, and therefore tragic, farewell.

The Razor's Edge

unnydale High's own literary magazine, *The Razor's Edge,* had a stellar year. We published six issues over the course of the school year, two more than ever before. Our content was expanded this year to include biographical and historical essays, in addition to the usual short stories and poetry.

But there was nothing usual about this year's crop of stories and poems. Kyle DuFours saw his short novel, *September Casualty,* serialized over our six issues, and is already working with a literary agent in New York to try to sell it to a major publisher.

Owen Thurman wrote "An Ode to Emily Dickinson," which was also published in an *e-zine* called *The Live Poets Society.* We had three separate stories receive awards from *Hangin' Magazine for Teens,* and one, Heidi Barrie's "The Horse You Rode In On," was chosen for the National Young Writer's Program, winning Heidi a $2000 scholarship to the college of her choice. Rhonda Kelley, Laura Egler, Scott Hope, and Freddy Iverson were all finalists in the Voices of Tomorrow contest.

Congrats to all of our contributors.

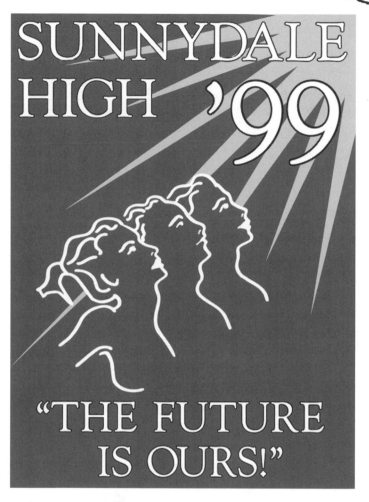

TOTALLY AWESOME!

SUNNYDALE HIGH '99

"THE FUTURE IS OURS!"

S.H.S. Yearbook

First of all, let's give a big Razorbacks' cheer to Mr. Baird, our yearbook advisor, without whom you'd probably be holding a bunch of Xeroxed pages in your hands. The most amazing thing about the yearbook this year, as in past years, is that it brings together a diverse group of people from the graduating class. This year we had athletes, performers, writers, and even a Homecoming Queen. (Actually, two of them!)

It's a huge undertaking, creating a book like this, but with so many wonderful people pitching in and doing their part, it didn't seem so much like work as it did one big party. So here's to the yearbook committee! We all have this beautiful volume with which to remember our years at Sunnydale High, and the committee deserves our thanks.

So, to Elliot Terhune, Michelle Blake, Lishanne Davis, Owen Thurman, Lisa Campiti, Holly Charleston, Mashad Bolling: great job, everyone!

GR-R-REAT!

Chess Club

The chess club had a very good year. Membership was up to a five-year high, and four club members participated in the Southern California Young Masters of Chess Tournament. They were Michael Czajak, Jason Kent, Jonathan Levenson, and Doug Jeffries. If not for the death of club president Andrew Hoelich just as school was getting under way this year, S.H.S. might have had a finalist in the tournament. Even so, the club did Sunnydale proud with its accomplishments.

Computer Club

Well, thanks to timely intervention by the computer club this year, S.H.S. is finally online with a smokin' website. Sure, we've had a site up for years, but in the wake of the tragic deaths of the club's advisor, Miss Calendar, and co-presidents Dave Kirby and Fritz Siegel, it had pretty much languished up until last spring, with the debut of the all-new, all-different Razorbacks Online. Dedicated to their memory, it took more than a year to fulfill the project's original goal. Laura Egler, Willow Rosenberg, and John Lee Walker put in lots of extra hours to make the dream a reality. Now, thanks to the club, S.H.S. alumni can look up the present-day whereabouts of fellow alums, and current students can look into various college programs and read alumni comments

about colleges and occupations. Teachers can post homework assignments online, and students can e-mail them in, as well as access work in progress they started on school computers.

Razorbacks Online.

High school will never be the same.

**"The printed page is obsolete.
The only reality is virtual.
If you're not jacked in,
you're not alive."
—Fritz Siegel**

When are we going to need computers in real life anyway?
—Xander

26

Dance Club

The dance club had a very busy year. Most of the first semester was spent learning about different choreographic styles. The club watched many dance videos, including Matthew Bourne's controversial production of "Swan Lake." Guest speaker Daphne Benedickt discussed job opportunities for dancers in the U.S. and Europe. Club members also hosted the Shalom Peace Project Dancers from Tel Aviv, hosting the guests in their homes during their two-day stay in Sunnydale on their tour through the U.S.

During the Winter Holiday, the dance club performed for the Sunnydale Rest Home, the Runaways Fund, and the Sunnydale Women's Club Holiday Bazaar. The spring dance recital highlighted works by Seniors Michael Czajak, Michelle Blake, Lysette Torchio and Harmony Kendall. Congratulations to Michael Czajak, who successfully auditioned for BalletWest. He hopes to join the company after graduation.

Drama Club

The hardest-working high schoolers in show biz had a banner year. The club organized and produced the school's productions of *Oklahoma* and *A Chorus Line,* with auditions open to the entire student body. No one who saw *A Chorus Line* this spring will forget the amazing performances put in by Scott Hope and Harmony Kendall. And who knows where Devon MacLeish got the energy (or the time off from Dingoes Ate My Baby) for his stint in *Oklahoma,* but we're all glad he did.

Owen Thurman directed John Mayhew and Holly Charleston in "Scenes from Shakespeare," which they performed for A.P. English classes last fall.

Still, there's no denying that the highlight of the year was the drama club's no-frills staging of *Cat on a Hot Tin Roof.* Heidi Barrie put in what the *Sunnydale Press* called "a heartbreaking performance —her pain seems all too real." Also receiving kudos was newcomer and jock Larry Blaisdell in his tremendous turn as Brick.

Another triumph for the drama club.

Math Club

Contrary to the image created by popular culture, the math club does a lot more than sit around solving complex mathematical problems and proving theorems. Several times over the course of the year, they solve complex mathematical problems and prove theorems in groups, with math clubs from other schools, in a kind of intense, scholarly competition that most people not in the math club would find it next to impossible to understand.

You don't need to know any of that. All you really need to know is that, thanks in particular to some of our standout students, Michael Czajak, Benjamin Straley, Chris Epps, and math club MVP Willow Rosenberg, Sunnydale High's math club kicked some serious quantitative and geometrical butt this year.

Congrats.

They sometimes have soda and snacks during the math. —X

Science Club

In December 1998, Sunnydale High School's science club played host to the regional science fair. Students attended from more than forty different schools from the surrounding counties. Science club president Eric Gittleson worked overtime to make sure that all the visiting students felt at home and that their projects were given the best showcase possible.

The projects placing first through third in the competition went on to the National Science Fair in Washington in March. Among those attending was our own Chris Epps, whose project, "The Human Body and How It's Built," received an honorable mention from the national judges.

Other Sunnydale High senior scientists were Amy Madison, Wendell Sears, Lishanne Davis, Roy Dukeshire, Amber Grove, Jason Kent, Jonathan Levenson, Willow Rosenberg, and Peter Clarner.

Cordelia, Tomato: Fruit or vegetable? —Willow

National Honor Society

The S.H.S. chapter of the National Honor Society had seventeen members this year, a greater number than any previous year in this decade! Willow Rosenberg and two-year-veteran Oz organized a Battle of the Bands to raise money for the Sunnydale Literacy Project.

The group also sponsored a tea for Breast Cancer Awareness Week, staged the first annual HIV study-a-thon, a grade-based effort to raise money for AIDS research and treatment, and a committee led by Chris Epps worked in conjunction with the S.H.S. chapter of Students Against Drunk Driving to plan the Mother-Daughter and Father-Son dinners in January.

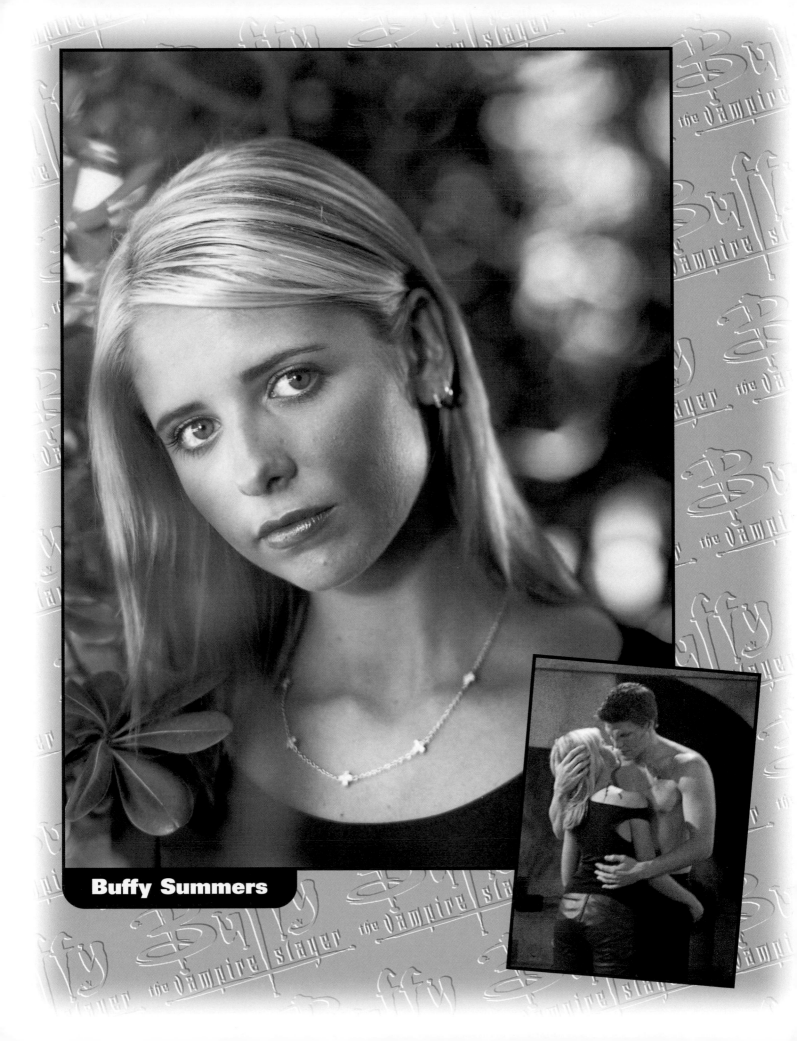

Buffy Summers

"You deserve more. You deserve something outside of...demons and darkness. You should have someone who can take you into the light."

—Angel

Angel

"In my world there are people in chains and we can ride them like ponies." —**Vamp Willow**

Willow Rosenberg

"I wished us into bizarro land and you guys are *still* together?"
—**Cordelia**

"They say that young people don't learn anything in high school nowadays, but I've learned to be afraid."
—**Xander**

Xander Harris

"See, in the end Buffy's good, but she's just the runner-up. I'm the Queen. If I get mad, what do you think I'm gonna do to you?"
—Cordelia

Cordelia Chase

Willow: "I feel different. You know... Do you feel different?...It's nice—was it nice? Should this be a quiet moment?"

Oz: "I know exactly what you mean."

Oz

Willow: "Promise me you'll never be linear."

Oz: "On my trout."

Giles

"**Buffy Summers,** Class Protector"

"I'm gonna go out on a limb here and say we've got a new Slayer in town." —Oz

Faith

Photography Club

The photography club was one of the most well traveled groups of S.H.S. students this year. In the fall, Guy Matthews, Hogan Martin, Scott Hope, Wendell Sears, and the rest of the club visited Balboa Park and the Gaslamp Quarter in San Diego, as well as Catalina Island, and in the spring, they went on the club's annual long weekend. This year's destination: the Grand Canyon!

Even better, photography club president and possible future king of the papparazzi, Eric Gittleson, won a *Seventeen* magazine student photography competition and had some of his pictures published in the magazine. So maybe there's something to the whole "art" thing.

Y'know, grab a camera, call it art, and it's amazing what you can get the school to pay for!

SADD

Students Against Drunk Driving had an extraordinary year, with thirty-seven percent of the student body among its membership, and more than twenty students on the events committee.

Thanks to donations from parents, teachers and others in the community, SADD was able to promote awareness of the dangers of driving under the influence of alcohol with posters, *S.H.S. Sentinel* ads, flyers at sports events, and even special events sponsored by our chapter of SADD.

Perhaps the biggest annual events held by SADD were done in conjunction with the National Honor Society. Thanks to Lishanne Davis, Harmony Kendall, and Percy West, the Mother-Daughter and Father-Son dinners in January were an even greater success in '99 than in years past. At these events, students and their parents sign contracts with one another, the students vowing never to drive drunk or ride with a drunk driver, and the parents vowing not to be angry or punish the students if they should call for a ride if they or their designated driver has been drinking.

More than anything else, we can be proud of this: in all likelihood, we saved lives this year!

French Club

Voulez-vous parlez avec nous? Led by Mr. DeJean, the French club took an occasional break from struggling with irregular verb form conjugations to savor *café au lait* and *éclairs* at their weekly gatherings. John Lee Walker, Doug Jeffries, Tor Hauer, Larry Blaisdell, and Lisa Campiti, among others, went out for a gourmet meal at L'Etoile, Sunnydale's new French restaurant. S.H.S. had a strong showing in the regional Frenchathon, with Lisa Campiti taking third place in the conversational category.

Latin Club

The Latin club is the largest language club on the Sunnydale campus. Maybe it's the toga parties . . . because S.H.S. does not offer Latin as a language. Still, seniors Lance Lincoln, Scott Hope, Michael Czajak, Amy Madison, Laura Egler, and Jonathan Levenson rarely missed a meeting. Asked why the popularity, club president Laura Egler said. "Gregorian chants and ancient magic spells are cool. Plus, we shout all the cheers at team games in Razorback (pig) Latin."

Ogay azorbacksRay!

Spanish Club

The *estudiantes del club español* had a year that was *muy divertido!* Selling tamales on Fridays, they raised enough money to send Kyle DuFours and Hogan Martin to the Diversity Forum in Los Angeles last fall. In addition, they played host to Enrique Delgado, S.H.S.'s foreign exchange student from Panama. On International Day, Katherine Wexford, Rhonda Kelley, and Heidi Barrie performed Mexican folk dances in the quad and supervised the breaking of a razorback-shaped piñata that they designed and created. The Spanish club also led a Christmas *posada* through downtown Sunnydale, finishing up with a fiesta at Our Lady of Peace Catholic Church.

A Message from Some Concerned Parents

1999 saw the creation of a new parents' organization in Sunnydale: MOO (Mothers Opposed to the Occult). MOO sought to eliminate certain inappropriate influences from the grounds of Sunnydale High School. Although the group got inexplicably out of control, a few of us have remained true to the cause. We are writing to urge those young people who leave S.H.S. this year to stay on the straight and true and good path to adulthood. Do not be tempted by promises of dark forces that yield power, wealth, and all the sex you can imagine. These things hold no lasting satisfaction! We ask you to look to us, your elders, and observe the joy we find in honest hard work. Stay the path, and you can become us! And isn't that better than some quick-fix fantasy world?

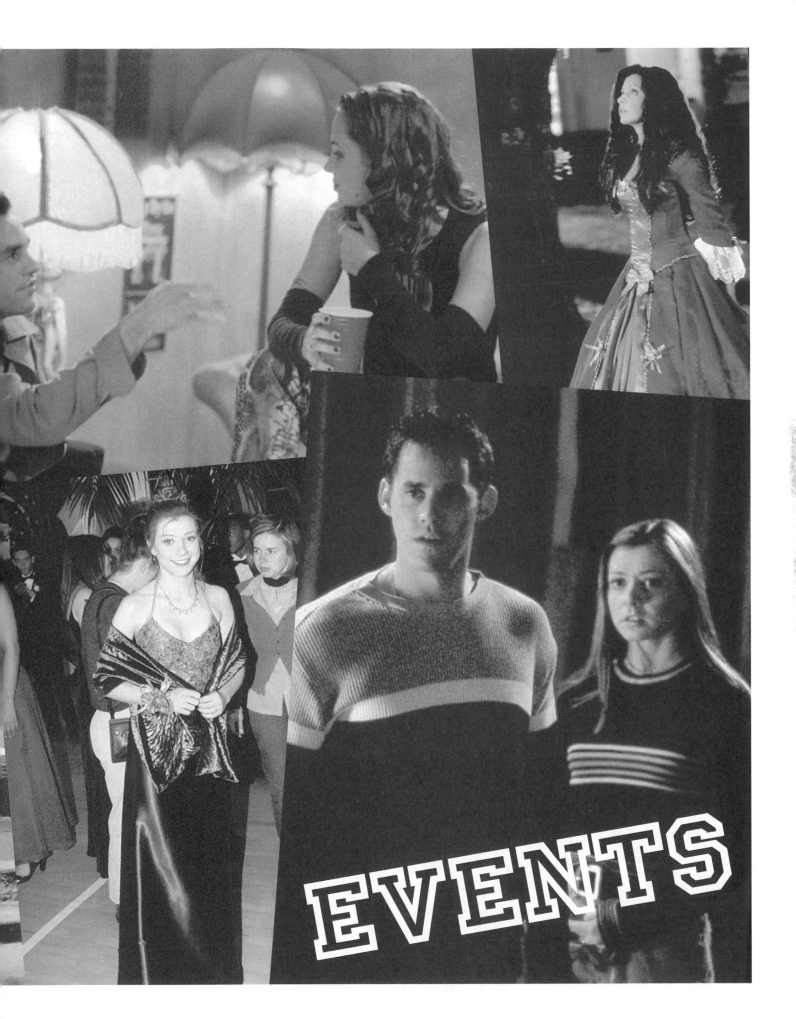

EVENTS

Halloween

NO BAD BOO! As usual, Sunnydale High showed its community spirit by participating in the "Safe and Sane Halloween" program. Organized by Principal Snyder, students escorted groups of menacing little demons, tiny wicked witches, and short but deadly vampires on this special night of tricks and treats. Ooh, check out those fangs! (Mrs. Davis, are you *still* giving out toothbrushes?)

The Espresso Pump awarded coupons for free coffee drinks and pastries to the winners of the school costume contest. First place went to senior Larry Blaisdell who came dressed as Judy Garland. Second place went to Harmony Kendall, for her Marsha Brady impersonation. And third went to Devon MacLeish, who actually dressed up! His Mick Jagger costume had everyone ROTFLT*O!

Career Week

Many companies and organizations came on campus for Career Week. They answered questions about entry-level positions and salaries and provided job applications for interested students. A number of employers who weren't represented last year (skittish after the accidental discharge of the law enforcement officer's service revolver the year before) returned to S.H.S. in '99!

When we have our ten-year reunion, it will be interesting to see how many of us are in the job fields we tested for. Maybe there's a Nobel prizewinner among us. Or the next Jewel—or Bill Gates!

The Foreign Exchange Program

Our favorite exchange student —Willow

Every year, Sunnydale High plays host to foreign exchange students from all over the world. The students stay in the homes of local Sunnydale families for two weeks. Razorbacks are very enthusiastic about the program. To quote senior Xander Harris, "I think the exchange student program is cool. It's the beautiful melding of two cultures."

The two-week visit ends with the World Culture Dance at the Bronze, where everyone dresses up in international costumes, as everything from Eskimos to hula dancers. Then it's "Adios" and "Sayonara" to new friends from far away.

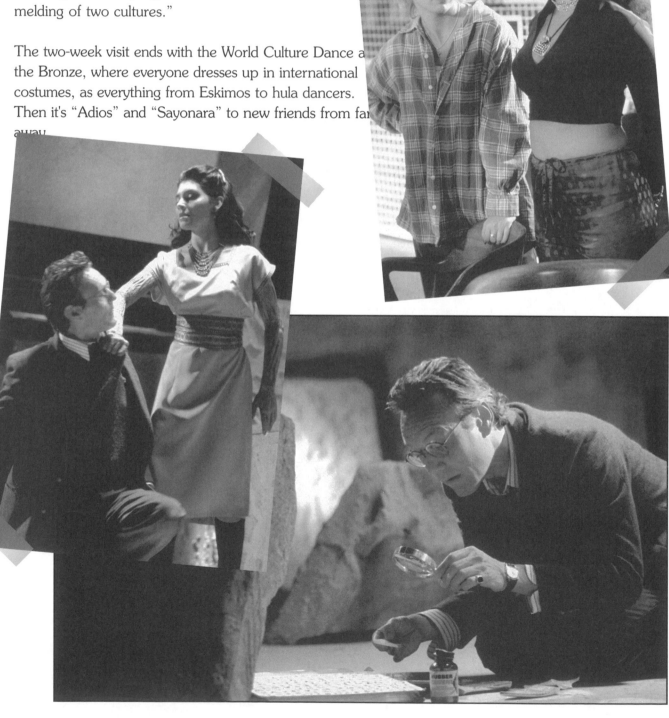

Talent Show

"There's no business like the business of show!" Mr. Giles was in charge of the talent show again this year, and he really outdid himself. More Razorbacks participated than in any other year—maybe because rehearsals took place during study hall instead of after school.

Well-known seniors who have performed in the talent show include Cordelia Chase, Lisa Campiti, Willow Rosenberg, Alexander Harris, Buffy Summers, Elliot Terhune, Lysette Torchio, Benjamin Straley, Gwen Ditchik, and Mitch Fargo.

Senior Scott Hope won first place for his solo of "What I Did for Love" from *A Chorus Line*. Second place went to Mashad Bolling, Roy Dukeshire, Tor Hauer, and John Lee Walker for their hilarious skit about four girls trying out for the position of head cheerleader in a wrestling match to the death, to the tune of "Be True to Your School."

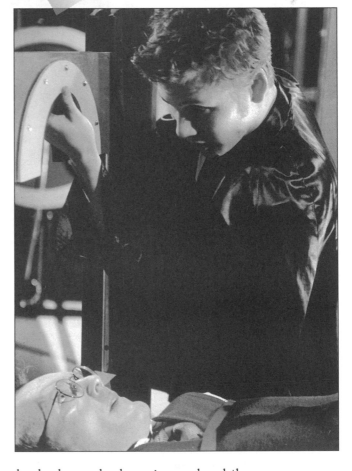

Third place went to Jonathan Levenson, who had everybody crying so hard they were laughing with his comedy routine about being "a moped-straddlin' geek!" Turns out Jonathan has a secret ambition to be a standup comic. Who knew?! Glad to see you back on track, Jono.

Sadie Hawkins Dance

In these liberated times, some feel that the girl-ask-boy Sadie Hawkins Dance has had its day. But it's been a time-honored tradition since the early '50's here at Sunnydale High. Last year, the dance was canceled because of a snake attack in the caf, but this year's dance went off without a hitch—unless you want to count the "hitchin' licenses" the Student Association sold as a fundraiser!

Do you realize that the girls are supposed to ask the guys—and pay and everything? I mean, whose genius idea was that?
—Cordelia

The Spring Fling

The traditional end-of-school dance was held, as always, at the Bronze. Triumphing over her defeat in her bid for Homecoming Queen, Cordelia Chase was crowned May Queen for the second time. (She was also queen in her sophmore year.) The Bronze was decorated with beautiful silk flowers and lots of tiny lights. Everybody had a great time dancing to the song stylings of Dingoes Ate My Baby and Four Star Mary.

**"Thank you. For making the right choice.
For showing how much you all love me...Being this
popular isn't just my right, it's my responsibility,
and I want you to know, I take it seriously."**
—CORDELIA CHASE'S ACCEPTANCE SPEECH

HANGOUTS

The Bronze

← They never paid us. –Oz

We're gonna party like it's . . .
DANCE TO THE MUSIC
1999!

Jammin' it in the gym on a Friday night after the football game . . . or not. But hey, where else can you get 7-Eleven–style burritos at jacked-up prices to share with your favorite chaperone? All together now: "Good evening, Principal Snyder! Are you stoked?" On the other hand, the bands were pretty good, sometimes there were free finger sandwiches, and the admission was about one-quarter what you paid at the Bronze.

For most people, the "mass and din" of the Bronze made it the only place to show. The infamous Senior Poll revealed that the majority of seniors would rather stay home and watch Hindu TV than be seen anywhere else (if they have to stay in Sunnydale!) on a Saturday night. Live music almost every night, mochaccinos, and total club ambience. Bye, bye, Miss Eskimo Pie—remember Willow Rosenberg's "hot" costume at the World Culture Dance last year?

As the Class of '99 moves on, and many leave Sunnydale for collegiate climes, the Bronze will be the measure by which we judge all future clubs . . . at least until we turn twenty-one and we have a little more to choose from!

Our Senior Poll revealed the most popular band of the Class of '99 to be (envelope, please!) Dingoes Ate My Baby. No surprise there. Sunnydale has always been loyal to the locals.

Now that's a rockin' year!

Special thanks to Claire Bellamy and Nick Daniels at the Bronze for hosting the wrap party for the S.H.S. Yearbook staff.

A failed attempt at a fourth chord. –Oz

The Point

Or "points," if we have to be specific. 'Cause there's more than one. These beautiful and secluded spots are the highlight of the nature experience in Sunnydale and offer quite scenic views. Of the town. Of the ocean. And in either case, there's no doubt that those views are that much more breathtaking at night, with the stars up above and the lights down below.

Very intimate.

When we wanted to go for a little drive—or maybe a long, slow drive in a vehicle with a powerful engine—to a place where the other people who've come to look at the view are involved enough with their own *looking* that they're not going to pay any attention to *our* looking, well, the Point is the ultimate destination.

Such a natural setting to do what comes naturally. There isn't a more exciting spot in all of Sunnydale.

The Espresso Pump

Okay, sure, we can all remember a time when Starbucks was nirvana for Sunnydale coffee lovers. Sshhhyeah! The fact that there was only *one* Starbucks was a major source of angst for most of us freshman year. Just regular old coffee wasn't enough, once we had a taste of what Starbucks had to offer.

Then along came The Espresso Pump, and our eyes were opened to a brand new kind of caffeinated heaven. It wasn't enough, now, to have good service and a splendiferous cup of some heady brew that began its brief life as just coffee, before the sorcerers at The Pump worked their particular brand of magic. Some might say, "It's just coffee."

Well it ain't.

Whatever you order, it isn't just coffee when you get it at The Pump. Every selection is an extraordinary and exotic blend of beans and assorted other ingredients. And where else would you want to hang, to schmooze, to gossip? We all felt at home at The Espresso Pump. It was our place in a way a chain-something could never be.

In the beginning, there was coffee.
Then coffee grew up.
Now, so have we.

The Mall

Go ahead. Lie. Say you don't hang at the mall. But make sure you have a smirk on your face when you say it, 'cause we'll know you're lying. Why?

'Cause we've seen you there.

Sure, nobody wants to admit it. We're all totally too sophisticated to be mallrats. But on weekends, when the sky dared to rain and the Bronze wasn't open yet, or when it actually—God forbid—dropped below sixty degrees and the beach didn't look like the best idea . . . yeah.

The mall.

Sure, it's filled with chain stores and sometimes the sprinkler system would go off inexplicably and things would blow up. And, lest we forget, the edibles at the food court barely fit the legal definition of the word. But drifting through the mall . . . not even shopping, not even buying . . . running into buds and making new ones, you can't deny we did all of that and more.

There are other malls. All over the country. All over the world. But this one will always be "the mall" to all of us. One of these days, "going to the mall" will just mean shopping. But for now, it still means something different.

See you there!

Playa Linda Beach

It's just "the beach." Sure, tanning hasn't been cool for years, but that didn't stop us from spending way too much time on the beach. There's a lot more to do on the sand than just tan, and the Class of '99 did it all.

Bonfires.

Volleyball.

Luaus.

Surfing.

Just plain old swimming, of course. And then there's all the things you can't tell your parents about. (You know what we mean, so we won't write any of it down here.)

Okay, so maybe the little stand at Playa Linda has the worst hot dogs of all time, but they make up for it with the greatest onion rings in the known universe. And maybe there are too many rocks, but the waves are the major bomb.

And the beach is drama, too. Think about it. How many times in the last four years did you break up or make up or hook up or look up at the stars and see one fall? Or look out at the waves and think you saw something big out there? How many fights did you have? How many times did you think about the future, and maybe even think that with the sun (or the stars) shining down and the waves rolling in, and the wind on the water, and friends laughing and music playing and a smile from someone special . . . that this was the most perfect moment ever.

The beach.

When we look back on our time at Sunnydale High, a lot of the memories that come to mind will have been made on the sand.

Putter's Green Mini-Golf

Admit it, we all love Putter's Green! Sure, maybe it hasn't been quite the same since your parents had your birthday party there in the fourth grade, or took your first date there in junior high, but in high school, we experienced a renaissance of interest in mini-golf.

When we all wanted to act like we were in junior high again, and pretend that college or work or just plain growing up was much further away than it actually was and is, what better place was there to go? Where else can you play through windmills and clown faces and pirate ships? Where else can you cheat and nobody cares? Where else can you go and be reminded of Homer and Marge Simpson doing it in public?

And don't forget, when it came to bonding with the 'rents, Mom and Dad liked mini-golf, too. While they were there, they could act as much like kids as the rest of us.

In fact . . . I think I'm going tomorrow. Anyone wanna come?

Hey, Buff! No cheating! And man...those cookies. Maybe we oughta get ol' Ted booted up again and hook him up to a mini-bake oven!
—Xander

48

The Sunnydale Zoo

Lions and tigers and bears! Oh my!

With its restaurants and walking gardens and petting zoo and everything else it has to offer, not to mention some pretty exotic animals, from pandas to panthers, the Sunnydale Zoo is second only to San Diego in the southwest. Part of the pride of Sunnydale, the zoo is nearly as old as the city itself, and never failed to entertain on field trips and weekend visits. Whether just to look at the animals, eat out, or go for a romantic walk, the zoo's second to none. And the bat cave and the spider house were always good for a few chills and thrills. Not only is the zoo a very cool place to bring a date, especially the first time around, it's a fun way to spend a day with friends, just hanging out, and it's so handy to the rest of town that it isn't a major trip to get there. With the family, friends, or a date, the zoo isn't just for animals!

I can remember a certain Sunnydale student acting like an animal at the zoo.
— Willow

Not fair, Will! Hyena possession, remember?
— Xander

Not THAT excuse again!!
— Willow

Sun Cinema

Yet another part of what makes Sunnydale the #1 place to live! Sure, other cities and towns have those huge, garish cineplexes, where the movie choices are limited to the latest Hollywood offerings.

Here in Sunnydale, we're lucky enough to have the Sun Cinema. Not that the Sun doesn't run Hollywood's latest crop—they do, but they've got so much more to offer!

Whether it was the all-night horror show, the animation festival, retrospectives honoring the films of Chow Yun-Fat or Jackie Chan or Buster Keaton or Humphrey Bogart, or even special double bills of movies with Abbott & Costello or John Wayne or Jim Carrey or Clint Eastwood . . . or Oscar-bound foreign films or silent classics or The Worst Movies of All Time . . . we were there. Some of us were in the balcony, or the back rows, where we maybe couldn't see as well, but we were there.

Whatever it was, it didn't matter.
The Sun Cinema is cool!

particularly during subtitled foreign language films.
— Angel

Hammersmith Park

Okay, maybe once upon a time, we would have put Weatherly Park in here instead. But ever since Hammersmith's renovation (and partially due to that certain breed of hungry locals who tend to frequent Weatherly), Hammersmith Park is #1! Every weekend is like the Fourth of July. With outdoor concerts, street performers, food, balloon vendors, Rollerbladers, and the skateboard pit, Hammersmith Park is *it*. This is what Sunnydale is all about!

Whether you're walking around the gardens or studying on the grass, maybe having a picnic or playing some Frisbee, Hammersmith is the place to be. To hang. To see and be seen. To exercise, even, if you feel like running or blading. To show off, if you skateboard.

With the gardens and the food and the people . . . yeah, every weekend *is* like the Fourth of July at Hammersmith Park. Now, if we could just do something about the tourists, we'd have it all to ourselves.

The Lot

Okay, so technically, it's a part of school. But whether it's before classes start, when the last bell rings, or—for seniors—during free periods, the #1 place we all spent time hanging out was the parking lot. Tailgating, blasting music loud enough to shatter the windshield, breaking off into the little tribes and packs that make up any high school class . . . that was the Class of '99, hanging in the lot.

Sunnydale's best and brightest on display!

Swim Team

BOYS' SWIM TEAM
On Our Way Back

The 1998–99 boys' swim team dedicated all of its meets to Coach Carl Marin and four of his top swimmers, who have been missing since last year. Dodd McAlvy, Gage Petrozini, Sean Mitchell, and Cameron Walker led the 1997–98 team all the way to the state semifinals. Everyone was looking to the Razorbacks to win the championship for the first time in fifteen years.

This year, the team was much smaller, but what they lacked in numbers—and meet wins—they made up for in school spirit. The new coach, Steve Lannes, says, "Give us another year, and we'll be back on top!"

BOYS' SWIM TEAM: Coach Lannes, Al Bristol, J.G. Lopez, Guy Nagy, Mark Chin, Stuart Henry, Ryan Kaas, Chris Cates, Nate Chandler, Jonathan Levenson, Wendell Sears, Benjamin Straley

MIGHTY MERMAIDS
Girls' Swim Led the School!

The girls' swim team made it to the California Interscholastic Federation (CIF) playoffs this year. They dedicated their meets to Coach Marin and the missing boy swimmers as well.

GIRLS' SWIM TEAM: Coach Harvey, Nicki DiNieri, Kat Verot, Jamie Dewees, Melissa Starbuck, Janice Bell, Shandra Latts, Bobbi Keirsy, Drew Stevenson, Hailey Martin, JoAnn Thompson.

Football

RAZORBACKS!
V-V for Varsity

The varsity football season was one of disappointment, but the thrill of the game was most definitely there. "I expect the best out of my players. One year the best could be CIF, the next year it could be last place in league. All that really matters is that they gave the game their best shot," Coach Stevenson says.

VARSITY FOOTBALL TEAM: Coach Stevenson, Coach Brannigan, Coach Cleater, John Lee Walker, Larry Blaisdell, Blayne Mall, Keith Castonon, Sonny Lucero, Ken Stout, Matt Estes, Lynn Brumley, Spencer Rider, James Gill, Nick Davis, DeWitt Jaekel, Gary Maxwell, Al Torres, Peter Esposito, Truc Ng, Sam Treater, Richard Boelhauf, Russ Luna, Dustin Haynes, Ryan Ishii, Alan A̶ ̶ ̶ ̶ ̶ed Jallisco, Norman Fines, Chris D'Amato, ̶ ̶ ̶ ̶ ̶ ̶ ̶ ̶ ̶ ̶ ̶ Mobley, Todd Cromwell, Will A̶ ̶ ̶ ̶ ̶ ̶ ̶ ̶ ̶ ̶ ̶ ̶ ̶ ̶ ̶ ̶ichael La̶ ̶ ̶ ̶ ̶ ̶ ̶ ̶ ̶ ̶ ̶ ̶ ̶ ̶ ̶ ̶ ̶s.

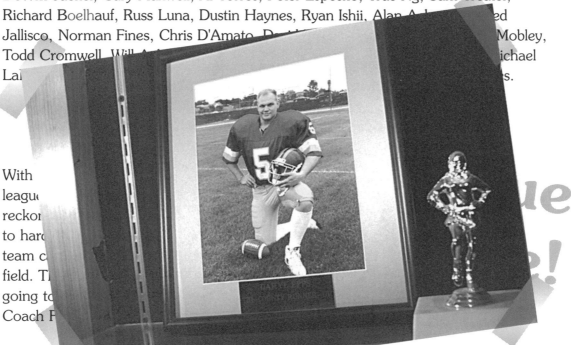

With
league
reckon
to hard
team c
field. T
going to
Coach F

JV FOO̶ ̶ ̶ ̶ ̶ ̶ ̶ ̶ ̶ ̶ ̶ ̶ ̶ ̶, Coach Lorenzetti, Coach Fine, Jake Ebbert, Jo̶ ̶ ̶ ̶ ̶ ̶ Ryan Neeper, Ronald Rickman, Jose Niero, Sonny Cardenas, Jeff Collins, Enersto Olvera, Nathan De Latour, Stephen Shrim, Kevin Makahili, Jack Cooper, Kory Santaigo, David Downs, Bob Smith, Marcellus Jackson, Stu Black, Scott Healy, Jerrod Moncreif, Lars Kojon, Ira Khabazian, Tom Holloman, Bert Metcalfe, Victor Clemons, Lee Shatzer, S. Jordan Livingston, Will Hess, Nick Cusumano, Jon Hickock, Keith Daily, Travis Kumerow, Brad Knowlton, Dave Ford, Dallas Hinchberger, Stan Hautala, Jason Van Adams, Rudy Ship, George Pines.

Basketball

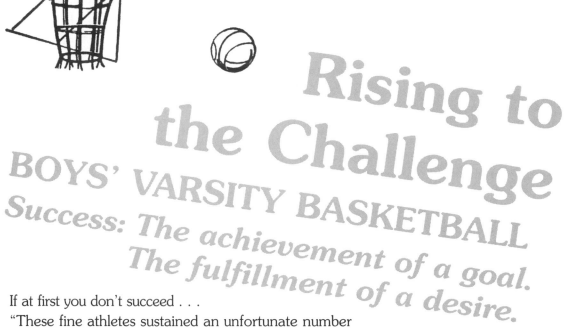

Rising to the Challenge

BOYS' VARSITY BASKETBALL

Success: The achievement of a goal. The fulfillment of a desire.

If at first you don't succeed . . .

"These fine athletes sustained an unfortunate number of injuries. I know that if some of our key players hadn't been sidelined, we would have brought home the CIF championship. Percy West's record of two division MVPs is something to be very proud of. And we're a stronger and more cohesive team because of the adversities we have faced," Coach Ellis says.

BOYS' VARSITY BASKETBALL TEAM:
Coach Ellis, Coach Sparkman, Coach Dominco, Percy West, Elliot Terhune, Andy Mativa, Josh Bagwell, Chris Dix, Ian Spell, Steve Chavez, Darren Maxey, Whitney Wolters, Jeimar Masada, Tom Hyux, Joe Rettingson.

Slam Dunk!
JV BRINGS IT HOME

The junior varsity placed first in the league for the first time ever! "This was the dream team of Sunnydale High. I'm very proud to coach such a fantastic group," Coach McAndrews says.

JV BOYS' BASKETBALL TEAM: Coach McAndrews, Coach Johannsen, Keith DeChanson, Jeremy Jackson, Bill Hightower, Ziven Vonk, Bill Browne, Andy Magnusen, Daniel Bootsworth, Jr., Corey Mariotte, Joe Harte, Stuart Wallace, Jamal Oyakoshi.

Killer Queens
GIRLS' BASKETBALL

Though the season was "stormy," teamwork and school spirit rate these girls an A for effort! "It was a challenging year for us, but so rewarding as well. Though we went without a win, the girls honed their skills and came together as a team. I'm looking forward to next year, when we'll put into play all the things we learned this year," Coach Carson says.

GIRLS' VARSITY BASKETBALL TEAM: Coach Carson, Gwen Ditchik, Katherine Wexford, Carly White, Ana McHale, Regan Motley, Katrinka Oviatt, Jaylynn Simons, Seska Carola, Karen Blick, Shoshanna Mandelbaum, Hillary Cavenaugh, Jeannie Jones.

These mighty maiden JV players kept their sights high and their goals in perspective as they built the team.

JV GIRLS' BASKETBALL TEAM: Coach Espino, Kenisha Esmenty, Michelle Gilmore, Ginjer Enche, Betsy Schuler, Amy Davenport, Davida Smotrich, Alisson Rabb-Macy, Torry Soloman, Trisha Duratt, Kelly Anderson, Yadira Ali-Man.

Baseball

**Varsity Baseball:
PUT ME IN, COACH!**

This year the team worked and worked and hung tough and ended strong. They went to second round of the California Interscholastic Federation playoffs and came home proud! "This was the best team I've been on. I'll miss playing with the Razorbacks. We're Number One!" player Larry Blaisdell says.

VARSITY BASEBALL TEAM: Coach Cholodenko, Mitch Fargo, Blayne Mall, Robert Stefanopoulos, Eric Meddings, Larry Blaisdell, Shane Jaekel, Marshall Irvin, Ryan Doak, Eric Struble, Eric DiNieri, Ronald Edwards, Ryan Pesaniello, Joe Jasslin, Wayne Caldicott, Albert Brouse, Anthony Wilson, Tony Sloan, John Willette, Ben Thurber, Scott Handley, Chet Smith, Arthur Thrifter, Jack Elsinore.

"As a team, we work together and play together. The players are there for you and help you through the rough times. Being on this team takes a lot of hard work and discipline. But together, we are Razorbacks!" says shortstop Aiden Brawley.

**JV Baseball:
Batmen!**

JV BASEBALL TEAM: Coach Briner, John Lindstrom, Scott Wilson, Anthony Cervantes, Rudy Lantz, Matt Petters, Josh Wilson, Dusty Hess, Ed White, Chris Whitaker, Mike Bonillas, Greg Goldstein, Aaron Schatzer, Ryan Valencia, Willy Brosel, Aiden Brawley, Josh Carter, Joe Final, James Peters, Jake Milam, Bryson Galvan.

Track

Leaders of the Pack!

Girls' track sustained an unusual number of injuries this year. Most of the seniors were sidelined, but they cheered on the team, showing true Razorback spirit. "The best thing about track is that it keeps you in shape while making you strong mentally. We're almost CIF material, if not this year, then next year. We will fly!" Lisa Campiti says.

GIRLS' TRACK TEAM: Coach Lemus, Lisa Campiti, Katherine Wexford, Evelyn Chipman, Tiffany Bee, Loeklani Bee, Tamara Treeter, Candy Trujillo, Ann Marie Gist, Natalie Butterfield, Feeleece Vargas, Shannon Mobley, Geanne Wilson, Jennifer Padilla.

Hit Me With Your Best Shot Put!

At the beginning of the season, boys' varsity track ran circles around the competition. Then some bad luck smacked into the team and a number of athletes learned the meaning of the phrase, "If Pain, No Gain!" Their spirits were high all season long, despite the setbacks.

BOYS' TRACK TEAM: Coach Bromm, Coach Monter, Elliot Terhune, Jeff Smith, Chris Vong, Reza Greene, Jared Floyd, Eli Stankevich, Jeremiah Fincher, Keith Cates, Gilbert Valles, Xavier Patino, Bobby Harrison, Josh Stuckey, Jason Hernandez, David Staley.

CROSS-COUNTRY Fleet Feet!

Pacing and speed are what cross-country is all about. Endurance and spirit to get to the end. Turbo-charged Razorbacks held their own this season, and Elliot Terhune went to the first round of the California Interscholastic Federation playoffs.

BOYS' CROSS-COUNTRY TEAM: Coach Jameson, Elliot Terhune, Scott Reed, Mark Simmons, Jonathan Castanon, Joe Burke, Tim Rohr.

GIRLS' CROSS-COUNTRY TEAM: Coach Smith, Lauren Yadilla, Olivia Winfree, Jeanine Howorth.

Wrestling

VARSITY WRESTLING

Thank You, Mat Men!

Our new coach, Coach Underwood, sent two wrestlers to the masters, and the team survived the hair-raising excitement of the state championships, placing in the top five slots! "Our wrestlers produced a lot of great effort by showing hard work and commitment to the team. We have a great future to look forward to next year," Coach Underwood says.

WRESTLING TEAM: Coach Underwood, Mashad Bolling, Roy Dukeshire, Tor Hauer, Guy Matthews, Robert Stefanopoulos, John Lee Walker, Jack Brawley, Larry Blaisdell, Leon Peppertree, Robert Galindo, Steven Williams, Jesse Nichols, Stuart Padilla.

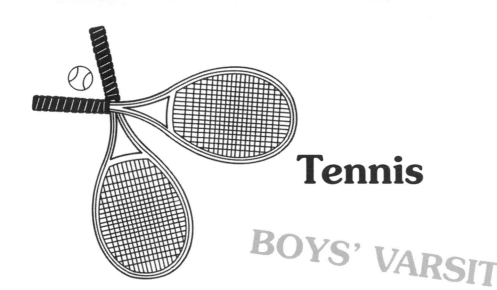

Tennis

BOYS' VARSITY TENNIS
Netting Success!

"Tennis is very competitive. It's a thinking man's game. I love the challenge," says senior Scott Hope. S.H.S. boys' tennis lost six seniors last year, so the team was a little smaller than usual. Coach John Smart says, "We know we'll build the team up over the summer, and we'll be back next year!"

BOYS' TENNIS TEAM: Coach Smart, Lyle Delaware, Alan Gram, Ryan Stevens, Tom Lagac, Ryan Tyler, Eric Gittleson, Scott Hope, Owen Thurman.

GIRLS' VARSITY TENNIS
Just a Little... Crush!

From last place to square in the middle, girls' tennis had much to be proud of this year. Coach Kevin Santiago welcomed Coach Dan Bacci halfway through the season.

GIRLS' TENNIS TEAM: Coach Santiago, Coach Bacci, Sally Tompkins, Monica Anderson, Georgiana West, Sarah Epperson, Linda Roberts, Tiffany LoDuca, Crystal Doyle.

59

Soccer

Wonder Women!

With hopes of reaching a league victory, varsity girls are SOCCER STUDS! Captain Holly Gill led the varsity girls to second place in the league, up from fifth last year. She says, "I am really, really proud of our team. These girls played hard and steady, and our record speaks for itself."

VARSITY GIRLS' SOCCER TEAM: Coach Donahoe, Rachelle Hearn, Holly Gill, Tamara Martin, April Calderon, Nicolette Perrson, Ashley Torrison, Lindsey Kaas, Nikki Sutter, Rachel Bouck, Julianna Lopez, Amanda Diece, Devin Henderson, Carly Gomez, Dana Darby, Lily Chow, Hiroyo Matsumoto, Jorgina Monte.

JV GIRLS:

Another season finished with the Razorbacks proud of their efforts. Placing fourth in league, they had a good time and worked very hard. Coach Cindi Gonzalvo says, "These girls really kicked it. They had a great season, and I'm very proud of them."

JV GIRLS' SOCCER TEAM: Coach Gonzalvo, Mary Bordon, Tiffany Castle, Beth Kukulic, N'cole Robinson, Kirsten Shaver, Aubrey Fratiani, Rosa Rosalez, Vonna Nadolson, Mae Chang, Ella Nguyen, Evelyn Clingan, Seana Embry, Rebeka Stigall, Regina Suave.

VARSITY BOYS

"The 1999 boys' soccer team is the best soccer team Sunnydale High has ever had. This team brought out fans and now it has respect. We were two-one in the CIF playoffs, and that's something to be very proud of," Coach Spacey says.

VARSITY BOYS' SOCCER TEAM: Coach Spacey, Mashad Bolling, Roy Dukeshire, Tor Hauer, Robert Stefanopoulos, Steven Hurtado, Bill Van Zanten, Dave Ledbetter, Anthony Crowell, Rodney Amlee, Eric Turrentine, James Davis, Steve Colvard, Jayson Ellis, Justin Trausch, Ryan Stockton, Jeimar Wakim.

"Graduation is a pointless ceremony where you sit around and listen to boring speeches till you get a little piece of paper that says you graduated which you already know and red does nothing for my complexion so don't argue, okay?" —**Buffy**

Spike and Dru

Kendra

"You look great, and you got the Barry working for you, and it's all good...." —Oz

"We're Slayers, girlfriend.
The Chosen Two."
—Faith

Angel: "Buffy, please don't."
Buffy: "Don't what? Don't love you? I'm sorry, nobody told me I had a choice! I can't just change—I'll never change. I want my life to be with you."

"At least I got to you two before you, you know, actually *did* anything."
—Buffy

"I'm over the whole 'Buffy gets a perfect high-school moment' thing. But no way am I going to let some subhuman rob the entire senior class of theirs." —**Buffy**

"You guys are gonna have a prom. The kind of prom everyone should have. I will give you all a nice, fun, normal evening…." —**Buffy**

"For God's sake man! She's eighteen and you have the emotional maturity of a blueberry scone. Have at it, would you, and stop fluttering about." **—Giles**

"Congratulations to the class of 1999. You've all proved more or less adequate. This is a time for celebration, so sit still and be quiet."
—**Snyder**

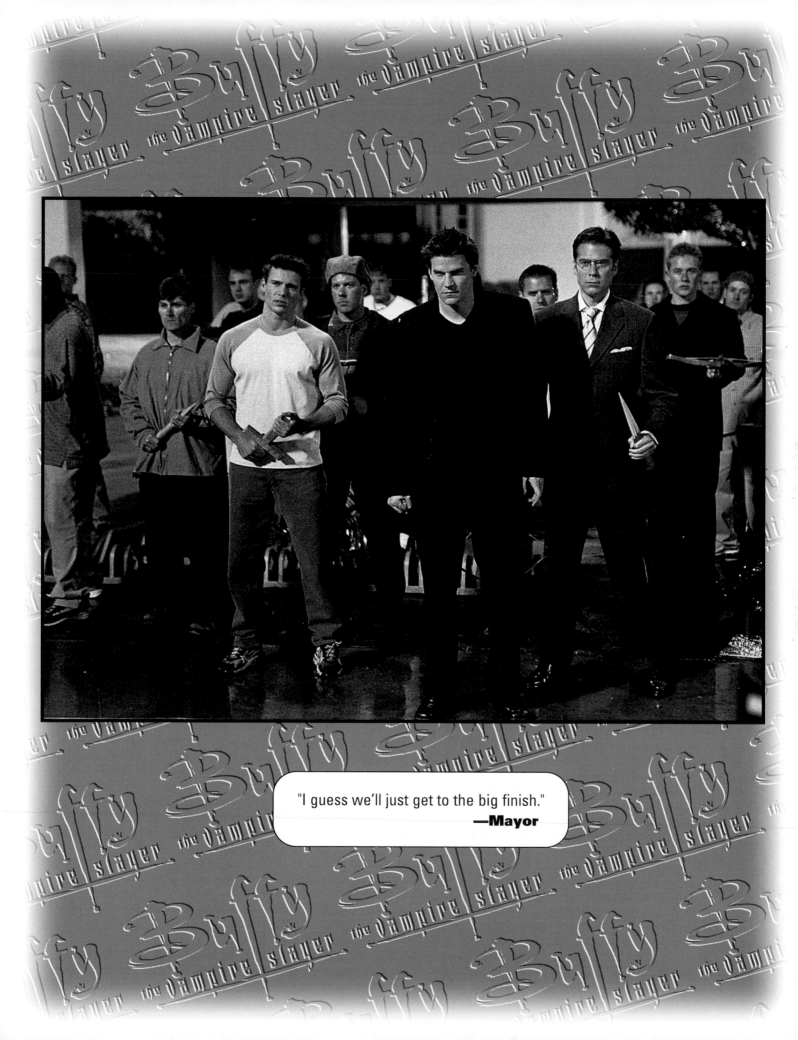

"I guess we'll just get to the big finish."
—**Mayor**

"Now we're supposed to be deciding what we wanna do with our lives and I realized that's what I want to do. Fight evil. Help people. I think it's worth doing, and I don't think you do it 'cause you have to. It's a good fight, Buffy, and I want in." —**Willow**

The boys' JV team tied for third in league, showing passion and commitment to their sport. The team was especially proud of their win against Rancho Dolores, which was their toughest competition this season.

JV BOYS' SOCCER TEAM: Coach Sandoval, Marc Grushen, Scott Wynn, Daniel McAlary, Robert Early, James Navarro, Mark Cooper, Paul Sotelo, Rithy Hepinger, Mike Milam, Sam Stevens, Phil Perez, Luis Ramirez, Dustin Torres, Juan Flores.

Field Hockey

The girls' varsity field hockey team dominated the league this year. They started the season strong and ended up even stonger. Girrrrrl Power! "These girls worked harder than any other team I've ever coached. It was a great honor to help them achieve their dreams," Coach Norman Jackson says.

Stick It Good!

GIRLS' FIELD HOCKEY TEAM: Coach Jackson, Harmony Kendall, Lysette Torchio, Silla Martin, Janet Black, Mare Fiedel, Amanda Chisholm, Eileen Lopez, Cathy Kennedy, Paula Jorgen, Yolanda Spencer, Tina Krieg, Rose Wendell, Nancy Kildare, Kristi King, Michelle Wentworth, Vanessa Scrivener, Carolyn Stiller, Janice Brown.

Gymnastics

BOYS' GYMNASTICS: A Perfect 10!

Dedication...

The boys' gymnastics team dedicated all their meets to Andr[ew] Hoelich, who died early in the beginning of the school year. Coach Zamudio says, "Andrew was one of the most agile gymnasts it had ever been my pleasure to work with. It's a terrible shame that his dream of going to the Olympics will never be realized."

BOYS' GYMNASTICS TEAM: Coach Marco Zamu[dio] Jack Sparks, Jorge Cross, Nathan Stockman, Michael Green, Todd Jones, Corey Sanderson, Michael LaPierre,

My Pain
a poem by Cordelia Chase

Everyone endures some pain
I hear each life must have some rain
But no one here wants to admit
That Cordy gets the worst of it.
Can't they look at me and see
The strain of being somebody?
In one short day, my love derailed
On top of that, I got impaled.
The stress that comes with being me
Is really, really B-I-G.
And no one even seems to care
That MY pain is much worse
than theirs.

Cheerleading

It was exciting to
have not one, but both Homecoming
Queens on the varsity cheer squad. Congra...
Michelle and Holly, no one deserved it more...

VARSITY CHEERLEADERS: Michelle E...
Lishanne Davis, Gwen Ditchik, Amber Grove,...
Zeiser, Britnee Brower, Robin Lee, Tiana Opu...

MASCOTS: Doug Gregory, Sean Maartins.

*"I love doing stunts. You have to depend on ...
look of awe on the faces in the crowd is worth...*

*"I've had some exciting times on the squad, tha...   ...people say I'm on
fire, first I look, and then I say thanks for the warning!"* Amber Grove says.

*"School spirit and charisma are essential as a cheerleader. Last year we weeded out
the girls without school spirit, and this year we showed people what cheerleading is all
about!"* Cordelia Chase says.

Just shout it
out! With their amazing stunts
and awesome routines, the JV
cheerleaders wowed them at
games and in competition. During a recent pep rally,
they really knew how to pump it up! Death-defying stunts made everyone gasp!

JV CHEERLEADERS: Amber Garner, Shauna Samuelson, Amanda Marcoux, Erika
Snider, Megan Blatter, Brittany Rodgers, Ka'cee McLeod, Cigi McCord.

FACULTY

Snyder's dream —Cordelia

Principal Snyder

"A lot of principals tell students, think of your principal as your 'pal.' I say, think of me as your judge, jury, and executioner."

Mr. Baird - *History*
"The secret of education is respecting the pupil."
—*Ralph Waldo Emerson*

Mr. Beach - *Geometry and Trigonometry*
"The shortest distance between two points is a straight line."

Ms. Barton - *Biology*
"When there is no wind—row!"

Miss Beakman - *English*
"No act of kindness, no matter how small, is ever wasted." —*Aesop*

Mr. Chomsky - *History*
"In a world of victims and executioners, it is the job of the thinking person not to be on the side of the executioners." —*Camus*

Mr. DeJean - *French*
   "A man travels the world over in search of what he needs and returns home to find it."—*George Moore*

Mr. Miller - *History*
"A people who don't know history have no past and no future."

Mr. Giles - *Librarian*
"I think the words 'let that be a lesson' are a tad redundant at this juncture."

Ms. Moran - *Sociology*
"There is nothing wrong with making a mistake at the beginning. The idea is to correct it before you are finished."

Mr. Herrold - *Phys. Ed.*
"The credit belongs to the one who is actually in the arena."

Ms. Murray - *English*
"The greatest honorific in the English language is the word 'teacher.'"

Ms. Jackson - *Math*
"Whatever women do, they must do twice as well as men to be thought half as good. Luckily, this is not difficult."

Miss Litto - *Phys. Ed.*
"Enjoy your life without comparing it to another."

Ms. Miller - *English*
"It is the greatest of all mistakes to do nothing because you can do only a little."

Mr. Nyman - *Calculus*
"Think."

Mr. Pole - *Driver's Ed.*
"Let's buckle up, people."

Who *is this guy?*

Style. Learn to recognize it. —Cordelia

Ms. Tischler - *Health and Human Services*
"Just Say No."

Mr. Whitmore - *Phys. Ed.*
"Wake up and smell the coffee!"

Mr. Taggert - *Chemistry*
"You don't have to have the lead as long as you have the heart to come from behind."

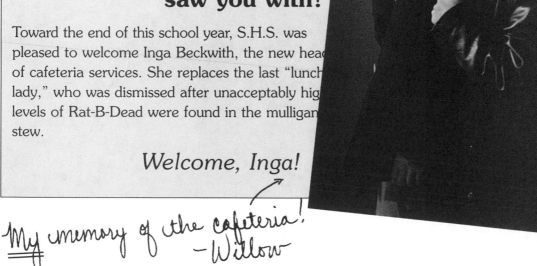

"Who was that ladle [ ] saw you with?"

Toward the end of this school year, S.H.S. was pleased to welcome Inga Beckwith, the new head of cafeteria services. She replaces the last "lunch lady," who was dismissed after unacceptably high levels of Rat-B-Dead were found in the mulligan stew.

Welcome, Inga!

My memory of the cafeteria! —Willow

You girls slay me. (sorry) —Xander

STUDENTS

This is how I love her best ... silent. -X

Heidi Barrie

"Crunchy."

Nicknames: Hi-ho, Didi

Activities: Spanish Club, *The Razor's Edge,* Drama Club

Memories: Most I'd rather forget; Tor, Ronnie, and Kyle—animal instincts; life is happier as a vegan; Quarters; superfreak; footballmen; beaching and blazing; prom night(mare); mallrat exterminators; the Bronze; Let it snow!; Lilith Fair.

Larry Blaisdell

"I'm so out I got my grandma fixing me up with guys."

Nicknames: Lorenzo

Activities: Football, Baseball, French Club, Drama Club

Memories: The stranger; Limo; rule #22 and #0; Folds; why can't this one fly; New Year's Eve Big Time; HGY's; Senior Six; Like you read about; John Lee and Mashad; Sunday Morning Practice; I owe you, Harris; Thanks, Dad.

Michelle Blake

"I have so many people to thank, I don't know where to begin."

Nicknames: Misha, 'Chelle

Activities: Cheerleading, Yearbook, Dance Club, Homecoming Queen

Memories: San Diego bound with Blayne & Alli-SIN!; SMK, BK, KJ, kiss me I'm me!; Charlie, HQ sister, "see ya, luv ya, miss ya already"; CC and BS and WHAT HAPPENED TO THOSE DRESSES? Catfight!!; Broom closets have more room than I thought!

Mashad Bolling

"It isn't about winning or losing, it's about looking good winning OR losing."

Nicknames: Potato head

Activities: Wrestling, Soccer, Yearbook, Jazz Band

Memories: DON'T call me "Butch"; wake me up for dinner; panty raid!; PB with Blondie and Harm; Lishanne, if you're ever lonely . . ;) . . .; damn the torpedoes; Matty on the mat; Coach, I just couldn't SEE the ball!; Mom and Dad . . . can I start over?

Lisa Campiti

"Truly great friends are hard to find, hard to leave, and impossible to forget."

Nicknames: Boo-Boo, Lissaboo, Tuba

Activities: Jazz Band, Concert Band, Yearbook, Track, Talent Show, Science Club, French Club

Memories: Berklee; MB, DR, AC, CF; We don't DO this one; Adv. Chem; Bones; Weatherly Music; Hot tub; Spring Fling; Mr. DeJean; Ms. Miller; hangin' at the Pump; beach bunnies!; thanks, Mom, Dad, Gramps, and Gram.

Holly Charleston

"Good times are never gone. There are always memories to look back on."

Nicknames: Charlie, Hollywood

Activities: Cheerleading, Yearbook, Drama Club, Homecoming Queen

Memories: HG, TY, RV, luv ya guys; Misha, HQ sister, "see ya, luv ya, miss ya already"; all night on the beach; zoo animals; mallrats; the Pump; the Bronze; Velvet Chain; talent show; Den 24/7; Shock the monkey; parents are kids in disguise—thanks, Mom and Dad.

Cordelia Chase

"I aspire to help my fellow man. As long as he's not smelly or dirty or something gross."

Nicknames: Cordy, Queen C

Activities: Cheerleading, Talent Show, May Queen

Memories: Harmony, Lishanne, Gwen & the girls; May Queen; prom madness; saving Ms. Miller's life (you're welcome!); love spells; Willow, thanks for the help; library fun with Mr. Giles and Buffy—boy, I love whittling! (note sarcasm); the Bronze; shopping with Mom!

Michael Czajak

"You can't begin to understand what's behind this face and mind."

Nicknames: Emcee, Warlock

Activities: Math Club, Dance Club, Chess Club, Tennis

Memories: Willow and Amy, kindred spirits at last—Blessed Be; who's my favorite rat-girl?; want some cheese?; the circle is open, and closed; Pythagoras was right!; dance fever (no tutus!); Andrew-K5 to Q3—Checkmate!!!; Dad, you believed in me. Love you.

Lishanne Davis

"We all get the spotlight eventually. You can have it when I'm done."

Nicknames: De-Lish-us, Lisha

Activities: Cheerleading, SADD, Yearbook, Science Club

Memories: CC; Amber's on fire!; Aura, Dan, Marc, Misha; "That's a burn;" Punkin Caper; LA w/ AG and CC; Betty pick up; Where's my camera?; MTV spring break in San Diego!; running the rat race; Mom and Dad and Allisyn, you're the bomb.

Gwen Ditchik

"It's nice skipping the small talk."

Nicknames: Guinevere, Gee, Digger

Activities: Cheerleading, Basketball, Talent Show

Memories: CC & the gals; Harm, Dally & tux guys; Hey Harm, the fleet's in, find me with the sailors; H! Miss ya, Suzy B!; beach baby; Herbert the pig; the Wahoos; Whammy; pattycakes; Amber's ablaze!; Mom & Dad, you're the best!

Kyle DuFours

"Everyone has the beast inside. For some, it's just a little closer to the surface."

Nicknames: 24, doofus

Activities: *The Razor's Edge,* Spanish Club

Memories: Rhonda, Tor & Heidi; don't even tell me what happened; the longest blackout on record; I'll never look at bacon the same way again; rathole; rocket fuel; Motel Six; swingin' on the Sun; career week—I should be a what?; No one here gets out alive.

Roy Dukeshire

"Put 'em up."

Nicknames: Dukes, Duke

Activities: Wrestling, Soccer, Science Club

Memories: Hangin' in the Lot with da Boyz; superfreak; "I don't think I can tell you that"; sophisticated lady—Amber! I love you; June bugs; Homecoming queensssss; prom night massacre; no it is NOT spiked, it's just punch—trust me!

71

Laura Egler
"I don't want to be left alone."
Nicknames: Egghead, Laurie
Activities: *The Razor's Edge,* Latin Club, Computer Club, Class Treasurer
Memories: Mitch, if you had any idea . . .; best of times w/ Kels, SM, DK, Suebee, and the men of the Bronze; spyder and me, sxl healing; "veni, vidi, vici"; jet-propelled love machine; one night in the Fish Tank and it's all over; see Dad & Mom, you survived!

Anya Emerson
"Men are evil."
Nicknames: Anyanka, Evil One
Activities: wishbringing, mischief-making, aiding in the vengeance of wronged women.
Memories: See above. Plus Xander.

Some demons have style, so what's all the others' excuse?
—Cordelia

Chris Epps
"Life's a puzzle. I just feel like I'm missing a piece."
Nicknames: Crisco
Activities: Science Club, National Honor Society, Math Club
Memories: Third and long, seconds to go. Where do you go? Number five. Daryl's gonna drive. I miss you, Daryl—I'm sorry; Eric; Willow; Buffy—who's smarter than she thinks; frog party; Kaos in Chem; I love you, Mom.

Mitch Fargo
"Libraries. All those books. What's up with that?"
Nicknames: None I'd care to repeat
Activities: Baseball, Talent Show
Memories: CK, MG, MN, MS (lotta M's!), I'm gonna miss dancing at the Bronze; the Point with Katie; Tijuana road trip, five days in stir; yes, ocifer; do you believe in ghosts?; up against the wall, MF; you call this a party?; M&D, you never missed a game!

Eric Gittleson
"No harm, no foul."
Nicknames: Skittle
Activities: Science Club, Tennis, Band
Memories: Six months in stir, and I still managed to graduate!; sorry Chris; sorry CC; I'm all better now, really; E. LeBeau; math w/ Mickey; Chem lab chaos; Dr. Gregory (moment of silence); Flutie-burgers; thanks Unc.

Amber Grove
"I'll bring the marshmallows."
Nicknames: Flygirl
Activities: Cheerleading, Science Club, Class Secretary
Memories: Go Razorbacks!!!; HI-C & Special K; "Stop Twisting!"; Keys under r.r.; Sha-fa; Benny's; Marriott w/ PD & SM; Room 202; Typical George question; Hey Ugly; Who's the cutest girl?; luvya mom+dad.

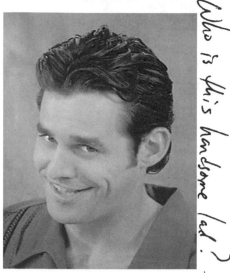

Who is this handsome lad? —X

Alexander Harris

"I laugh in the face of danger. Then I hide until it goes away."

Nicknames: Xander, X-Man, King of Cretins

Activities: Swim Team 3, Talent Show

Memories: The Scooby Gang; CC; Willow & Buffy; Oz; Amy; hangin' in the stacks with bad boy RG; Ho-Ho's; hyena days; Private Harris; Ampata; Faith; The Bronze; Jesse, I won't forget; please don't anyone mention Valentine's Day; Nighthawk; thanks for the loan, Uncle Roary.

Tor Hauer

"Pork. It's the other white meat."

Nicknames: Tor-nado, Toro

Activities: Wrestling, French Club, Soccer

Memories: Tijuana cerveza and Cuban cigars; the zoo crew, Kyle, Rhonda, and Hi-ho; superfreak; beaching and blazing; Lilith Fair; snowball fights at Hammersmith; Bronze potential; "Tor like women!"; mallrats!

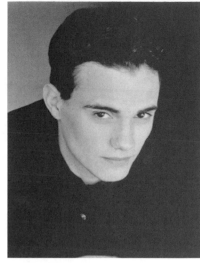

Scott Hope

"I'm a bad liar. It's not good for the soul."

Nicknames: Scotty, Scooter

Activities: Drama Club, Photography Club, Latin Club, *The Razor's Edge*, Tennis

Memories: Debbie & Pete, I miss you guys; Buffy, sorry to say I'm just a guy; what do you do for an encore?; International Day; Espresso Pump; festivals at the Sun; under the sea!; Mom, Dad, and Kristen, love ya!; I still remember a place called . . . nah, too easy.

Frederick Iverson

"Grades are meaningless."

Nicknames: Freddy

Activities: *S.H.S. Sentinel*, *The Razor's Edge*

Memories: NV, JG, WR; The Bronze; Inca mummy exhibit; late night trash talk turned into top notch column topics; get out of the herd and see the world as it is; I meant every word!

Douglas Jeffries

"Don't look back."

Nicknames: Doug, DJ

Activities: Soccer, Chess Club, Spanish Club

Memories: Lisa, wish I'd had the guts to tell ya . . . ; JK, dynamic duo; Lot Lizards; Knight to Queen's Four; L, yo digo te amo; I'm tellin' ya, I can play goal!; hey D, nice legs!; I wish they all could be California girls . . . oh, wait, I guess they are!

Rhonda Kelley

"What a tangled web we weave."

Nicknames: Ronnie

Activities: *The Razor's Edge*, Spanish Club

Memories: Quarters; superfreak; Heidi, girlfriend; Kyle & Tor; footballmen; Frankie; beaching and blazing; prom night(mare); mallrat exterminators; Time Warp weirdos; the Bronze; Let it snow!; nuggy kitty; Lilith Fair.

Harmony Kendall

"They can do wonderful things with airbrushes these days"

Nicknames: Blondie

Activities: Dance Club, Drama Club, Field Hockey, SADD

Memories: Hi CC, PV, CM; Mashad, don't pull my hair!; Chemistry Thucks!; John Lee, football hero!; Chuck S.; Christopher, I'm gonna kill you; Erin O., have a good year; Hey, give me those keys!; don't you dare!; prom madness.

Jason Kent

"Today is the first day of the rest of my life . . . I'm outta here."

Nicknames: Jace, Clark

Activities: Soccer, Chess Club, Science Club

Memories: Hey D! nice legs!; Amy M., any interest in a summer fling?; DJ—Rook to Knight's 3; dynamic duo; Wendell, is your experiment supposed to be on fire?; Juniper Hill, trolling in Hammersmith, beach bombs; love ya, Mom and Dad!

Jonathan Levenson

"I think you'll be impressed. It's the Cadillac of mopeds."

Nicknames: Jono

Activities: Science Club, Latin Club, Chess Club, *S.H.S. Sentinel*, Swim Team

Memories: Steam baths; thanks Xander & BS; so yeah, I peed! So what?; Jackie; Catch a Rising Star; zombie party; something weird's goin' on here; Cadillac; Good ol' boys; Napa Valley Bike Tours; Gondola; ninja boy; I'm still here, Mom and Dad.

Lance Lincoln

"Get your filthy paws off me you damn, dirty ape!"

Nicknames: Lance Link

Activities: *S.H.S. Sentinel*, Latin Club

Memories: Stop the presses!; Lois and Clark; "I'll be a monkey's uncle."; what's the name of the game?; if you don't know the answer, make it up; JG, FI, NV, WR . . . let's not forget those wonderfully cooperative Sunnydale peace officers; the truth is out there!

Devon MacLeish

"She doesn't have to talk."

Nicknames: Dev, Ol' Blue Eyes

Activities: Yeah. Right.

Memories: Dingoes; hometown crowds at the Bronze; Cordelia—you're still on my mind; the absent-minded guitar man; Seattle's dead; practice in the green room; Granny's ghost; Kathy, Stacie & Baker, time to finish what we started.

Amy Madison

"Within each of us is the power to change the world; all we have to do is let it out. Of course . . . some of us should leave it right where it is."

Nicknames: Mad-woman

Activities: Latin Club, Cheerleading

Memories: Michael and Willow, thanks for sharing; Blessed Be; no more cheese!; brownie parties; Xander, now I've got dirt on you!; toil and trouble; thanks to Mr. Giles and to BS; I love you, Dad.

I hope she'll look like this again soon. ~W

74

Blayne Mall

"Nothing wrong with an aggressive female."

Nicknames: Blayne-o, Blayne Damage

Activities: Football, Baseball

Memories: sufferin' b-tards w/ John Lee, Bobby & Mashad; scamming the Lot and Hammersmith; Roger's hellride; Doubles; Crawls; 3-27 w/Jackson; JJFlash in 3/4; Jelly; the Villa; Fuzzy Duck; B-Day w/ Jules. Mom and Dad, you're the best.

Hogan Martin

"Winning isn't everything . . . okay, so I'm lying."

Nicknames: Hoagie

Activities: Basketball, Spanish Club

Memories: double dribble!; West on the rebound—uh-oh!; H&L—bookends!; game high 36; division mvp x3; PW, FG, CH, NR, "Gentlemen! Off the bench and on the wood!"; hey Gwen-evere, let's talk Excalibur!

Guy Matthews

"Don't make me do something you'll regret later."

Nicknames: Matt, Matty

Activities: Wrestling, Photography Club, Wrestling, oh, and did I mention Wrestling?

Memories: Boyz Clubz of America!; hangin' in the Lot; the Point with AF; Espresso Pump; International Day—of course this is what they wear in Greenland!; watchin' the gals go by at Hammersmith Park; Den 24/7; damn the torpedoes; luv you, Mom.

John Mayhew

"Death and taxes are serious business; everything else is comedy."

Nicknames: Jack, Chewbacca, Animal

Activities: Drama Club, Baseball, goofin'

Memories: Bobby, Larry & Mitch, the infield of dreams; *Oklahoma!!!*; Larry, dude, "not that there's anything wrong with that," but you're not neat or thin enough, y'know?; HEY!; hopped up on the goofballs!; turn on anything, you'll get it; You want funny? A monkey in a diaper, now that's funny!

Me

Always cute –Oz

Oz

"I mock you with my monkey pants."

Nicknames: The Great and Powerful

Activities: Jazz Band, National Honor Society, otherwise as little as possible except playing with Dingoes Ate My Baby

Memories: Willow; full moon fever; Dingoes; Willow; Sweet J; looting military installations—just kidding!; Willow some more; the Chosen One et al; the five year program; punching Xander (sorry, man, but it was fun); getting shot sucks; hey, Mr. G., thanks for the chains; thanks Uncle Ken, Aunt Maureen, and Mom and Dad.

♡♡ *wwww – Willow*

Willow Rosenberg

"Don't warn the tadpoles."

Nicknames: Will, Brainy Smurf

Activities: Math Club, Science Club, Computer Club, substitute teaching, Talent Show, National Honor Society

Memories: Oz; Buffy & Xander, I love you guys; Amy & Michael; Cordy—"they're only men, they don't know any better"; Jesse and Ms. Calendar; thanks to the tutor's tutor, Mr. Giles; no more computer dating; ghost girl!; Chirayoju; Carpe Diem; Dragon's Cove; Bronzin' with the Dingoes; thanks, Mom and Dad.

75

Marcy Ross

"Have a nice summer."

Wendell Sears

"A wise man knows everything; a shrewd man, everyone."

Nicknames: When

Activities: Band, *S.H.S. Sentinel;* Photography Club, Science Club

Memories: What're you, Einstein?; Yes, Miss Rosenberg; WR, TK, JR, DO; dizzy devils; Weatherly; prom dates!; mini-golf; we ain't all on *Baywatch,* chica!; we coulda been contenders; I hate long good-byes, so . . .

Robert Stefanopoulos

"Time o' your life, huh kid?"

Nicknames: Bobby, Stef, Sundance

Activities: Baseball, Wrestling, Soccer, *S.H.S. Sentinel*

Memories: Marie 4 eva; Den 24/7; panty raid!; damn the torpedoes; blow up the chess club; "put 'in ____ ____ heer up ____ ____ ashad, ____ ____ ____ ____ t

Think I'll save the world today

Benjamin Straley

"Gallop through every sunset, but slow down long enough to watch it rise."

Nicknames: Ben, Benny, Stray

Activities: Talent Show, Math Club, Swim Team

Memories: Hellride w/ Roger; Crossfire; Q.; Cobby's; hang the mustang; "Flash" by the Chipmunks; Black Thursday—"no need for the piece"; Joke; Chesapeake; the Villa; "it's a classic"; damn the torpedoes; Den 24/7; Mom and Jeannie, love you both!

Buffy Summers

"If the Apocalypse comes, beep me."

Nicknames: Buff, Chosen One

Activities: Talent Show

Memories: Willow & Oz; Xander (nice Speedo); Queen C.; love that brooding guy; moon pies; Bronzing; Homecoming; Amy; ratface hopped up on band candy; bloodsucking freaks; snow on Xmas; Kendra and Ms. C., I miss you; thanks "Ripper" (okay, maybe you're not quite so stuffy after all); love ya, Mom & Dad.

Elliot Terhune
"Life is a poor spectator sport."
Nicknames: Ness
Activities: Cross Country, Track, Basketball, Yearbook, Talent Show
Memories: ET, JC, MH, PT & WN; bearcubs; La Jolla chicos; Camp Hoss; TB parties; Peter Gunn; Triathalon; flawless hoop; suicides; Volkswagen crash; Bill's bets; Grif impression; Gov; Slime Fireball.

Owen Thurman
"I never thought that nearly getting killed would make me feel so alive."
Nicknames: O.T.
Activities: Drama Club, Tennis, Yearbook; Class President
Memories: Emily D.; hit one in the windmill; the morgue—my best date ever; tailgating in the Lot; St. Pat's; Sailing; Pacific Beach; Thumper; Bear; MGB; Black Thursday; "Like the car, officer"; Flash; La Cucina; attaboy!; it's safe, Mom, really.

Lysette Torchio
"Smile. It gives your face something to do."
Nicknames: Torch, Lissa
Activities: Cheerleading, Talent Show, Dance Club, Field Hockey
Memories: Okay, Chase, you in or you out?; Harmony, Aura, Lishanne, girls on parade; hanging at Hammersmith; ladies' night at the Bronze; beach bunnies—I look good in this suit!; what your mother should know; never mind, Mom and Dad; love you, Troy.

John Lee Walker
"You only live once. But if you do it right, once is enough."
Nicknames: My mother named me John Lee, and that's what you'll call me.
Activities: Football, Computer Club, French Club, Wrestling, Class Vice President
Memories: Da Boyz are back in town; Bobby, Dukes, and Mashad; Harm; Sorry CC, maybe another time?; Den 24/7; once upon a time; girl o' my dreams; dance club girls, call me, we'll do lunch; oh, and Coach—I quit, baby. I'm goin' to Hollywood.

Percy West
"Hey, I'm challenged."
Nicknames: none
Activities: Basketball, SADD
Memories: put me in, Coach!; double dribble!; Harmony & Lishanne, my favorite bookends; game high 32; division mvp x2; HM, CH, FG, ET, NR, got your back, boys, get off the bench and on the wood; hey, Rosenberg, thanks for making me study.

Katherine Wexford
"The sound of a friend will be heard above the noise of life."
Nicknames: Katie, Kat-woman
Activities: Track & Field, Basketball; Spanish Club
Memories: Ahhh, memories!

Biggest Attitude

Harmony Kendall & Blayne Mall

Best Smile

Mashad Bolling & Michelle Blake

Best Dressed

Mitch Fargo & Amber Grove

Best Eyes

Amy Madison & Michael Czajak

Biggest Flirt

Devon MacLeish & Holly Charleston

Nicest

Scott Hope & Lisa Campiti

Teacher's Worst Nightmare

Tor Hauer & Rhonda Kelley

Most Likely to Be Famous

Cordelia Chase & Jonathan Levenson

Most Athletic

Larry Blaisdell & Lysette Torchio

Most Likely to Be Imprisoned

Buffy Summers & Kyle DuFours

Best Personality

Ben Straley & Gwen Ditchik

Cutest Couple

Willow Rosenberg & Oz

Looks & Books

Owen Thurman & Lishanne Davis

Class Clown

Jack Mayhew

Class Protector

Buffy Summers

SUNNYDALE HIGH • STUDENTS

In Memoriam

Principal Robert Flutie

"Bob Flutie was a compassionate man. His office door was always open. That's what got him killed."
—Principal Snyder

Mr. Stephen Platt - Guidance Counselor

We trusted him, and we miss him.

Kevin Benedict

We will not rest until we have justice in his memory.

Miss Jenny Calendar

Every student's dream teacher; every principal's nightmare. We loved you, Ms. Calendar.

Miss Ellen Frank

She always had time for a question, and never left a student in the dark.

Peter Clarner

A gentleman, a gentle soul, now with the one he loved the most.

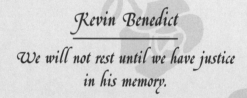

Dr. Stephen Gregory - Biology

More than any other teacher, he inspired us to want to learn.

Emily Djiemanowicz

The world has been deprived of her talent.

Debbie Foley

Losing her has taken some of the
music from our lives.

Andrew Hoelich

He dreamed of being a champion,
when to us he always was.

David Kirby

His legacy is a lesson: there is no burden
so great that it can not be shared.

Theresa Klusmeyer

There were no strangers to her, only friends
she had yet to meet.

Sheila Martini

We will always wish
for another chance to
understand her.

Jesse McNally

His smile and self-deprecating
sense of humor brought a little light
into all our lives.

Rodney Munson

He never stopped trying to improve himself
—a lesson for us all.

Jack O'Toole

He tried so hard, for so long,
but graduation eluded him.
You've made it now, Jack.
Time to rest.

Seems kinda weird not to have Larry and Harmony and Principal Snyder in here! Guess I just thought I should mention them. We stopped the Mayor, but those three paid the price. For all their faults, Larry and Harmony came through in the end.

—Willow

Morgan Shay

His dry wit and quiet intelligence will always be remembered fondly.

Fritz Siegel

His death is a great loss to the future of technology.

Jeffrey Walken

Every game the Razorbacks played this year was for him.

Dodd McAlvy, Cameron Walker, Gage Petronzi, and Sean Dwyer

Water seemed almost their natural element. Though they didn't live to take home their trophy, we have faith they have received their eternal reward.

Herbert the Pig, School Mascot

He had the heart of a fighting Razorback.

83

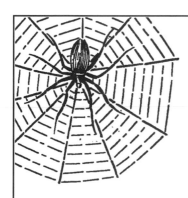
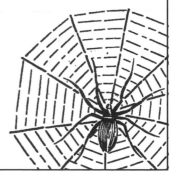

SUNNYDALE HIGH • ADS

86

JONATHAN—You are the sweetest, cutest, most intelligent, and funniest guy in our class, and nobody knows it, not even you. Well, except for me. I'm trying to get up the courage to tell you how I feel on graduation day. I hope I can.
—*An Admirer*

EGGHEAD—*Veni, vidi, vici! Carpe diem! And all that Latin crap. I'll miss your smile.*
—*Lance*

TO THE CLASS
WITH CLASS
John and Mary Jane Blake

KYLE—We wish the best of life for you.
Love, Mom & Dad

Good luck, Mitch.
Love, Mom, Erin, and Gran.

**To the class of 1999,
and especially our daughter, Amber:**
Believe in yourself and dare to live your dreams.
Love, the Grove Family

Buffy, no mother has ever been as proud. With all you've been through, your accomplishments are all the more inspiring.
—*Mom*

Best wishes and Godspeed to you all.
—*Arthur and Carol Terhune*

JOHN LEE—This is only the beginning of what life holds in store.
We love you.
—Dad, Mom, and Ashleigh

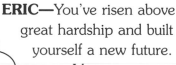

To all those who remember our son fondly, his spirit soars with you.
—*The McAlvy family.*

CORDELIA—We knew you were beautiful, darling. We just never realized you were so smart!
Love, your mother

HOLLY—The future is whatever you make it, honey. We love you.
—*Mom & Dad*

AMY—You're something else, kid. Wherever you lead, I'll follow. I'm so proud and happy for you.
Love, Dad

OZ—We know you wouldn't want us to make a big deal out of it. Big surprise. You take everything — and we mean everything — in stride.
But we just couldn't let this go by without saying "congratulations."
With our love and respect,
Uncle Ken, Aunt Maureen, and Jordy

ERIC—You've risen above great hardship and built yourself a new future.
I love you.
—*Nana*

CHRISTOPHER GOLDEN graduated from Marian High School in Framingham, Massachusetts, where he frequently disrupted the easily-diverted Mrs. O'Halloran's English class with discussions of movies or the previous night's TV lineup. Chris has painful memories of the talent show and what passed for baked manicotti in the cafeteria. He spent several years singing badly for a rock cover band called Crossfire. His favorite teachers were usually those he annoyed the most, including Father Hughes, Mr. Geary, Mr. Herlihy, and (oddly, since he despised Math) Mrs. Knapp and Mrs. Connearney (both of whom were also, not coincidentally, easily diverted from class work).

Go Mustangs!

Navy brat **NANCY HOLDER** went to three different high schools: Nile C. Kinnick in Yokohama, Japan ("Yo-Hi") and Vista High and Grossmont High, both in Southern California. At Yo-Hi, the school was so small that the student body had to vote between having a football team or a band (football prevailed). The number-one football cheer went like this: *Iki, iki, ikimasho!* Her favorite class was modern dance, because she didn't have to wear a gym uniform. On Grad Nite at Disneyland, she misplaced her contact lenses, got lost, and spent three years living on Tom Sawyer's Island eating nuts and berries. She was rescued by dashing Grossmont graduate Wayne Holder, and they got married.

Grossmont Foothillers Rule!

Have a nice Summer! ♡ Erin D.

Have a nice Summer!
Karen C.

Tina D

Cynthia J.

Yo'll Have A Nice Summer!!
Scott J.

Have a nice summer!
- Nicol O

Mike B.

Elise

Dave L

Lois G.

Joan M

Jane Y.

Have a nice summer!
Tone :)

Mike

Mark B.

Dick D.

Carol F.

Have a nice summer!
Dodger10.

Elaine B.

Luna

jane K

Gail P